Janet Smith

K6

ERIC AND THE LITTLE CANAL BOAT

By Lillian Bason

Illustrated by Anne Rockwell

PARENTS' MAGAZINE PRESS · NEW YORK

OTHER BOOKS BY LILLIAN BASON

Isabelle and the Library Cat
Pick a Raincoat, Pick a Whistle
Castles and Mirrors and Cities of Sand

To Roger with love

The little canal boat waited at her lakeside landing, clean and sparkling in the morning sunshine.

The boat landing was at the end of a winding path.

Soon the captain came walking down the path from his house. He had on a white uniform and a captain's cap, and he had a neat little black beard.

Next, the cook came down the path from his house. He had a round face and wore a white shirt and a white cook's hat and white trousers.

Then the boy who worked on the boat came running down the path, afraid of being late. His name was Eric, and it was his very first day of working on the boat. Eric wore a bright red shirt and old blue pants held up with a rope belt, and he was barefooted.

The engineer, in his blue overalls, was already below the deck in the engine room, polishing the gauges and getting the engine shiny and bright.

Soon the passengers came walking down the path, carrying bundles and suitcases and babies and cameras. Some were going to the town from their farms. And some were travelers who had come for the boat ride along the canal.

The captain called Eric to the wheelhouse. "Eric," he said. "This is your first day working on the canal boat. If you do a good job you can work all summer."

Then the captain said, "There are two things to remember. *The boat must always be on time, and the passengers must always be happy!*"

The captain turned back to the wheel and then he sounded the bell telling the engineer to start the engine.

Eric went all around the boat very fast, putting four fenders, made of wood with loops of rope, over each side, to protect the little boat on its way.

The captain called out, "Cast off!"

Eric hurried to unfasten the ropes at the bow and threw them on the landing. Then he ran back to the after deck, trying so hard to hurry that he got the rope tangled around his foot as he was unfastening it. He didn't want to do something wrong right at the start of the trip that would make the little boat late.

Just as Eric got the rope untangled, the captain looked at the boat's clock, signalled to the engineer, and the little canal boat was on her way, right on time.

The little boat was white, and looked very gay with brightly col-
ored flags flying from the mast. And at the stern was the yellow and
blue flag of Sweden. Along the ropes from bow to stern were flags of
red and white, white and blue, blue and red, all of them different, wav-
ing in the breeze.

Eric leaned against the rail as the little boat started across the
wide lake, her engine chugging. Along the shore he could see cows
in the fields, a farmhouse or two, and then a dark green forest of fir
trees.

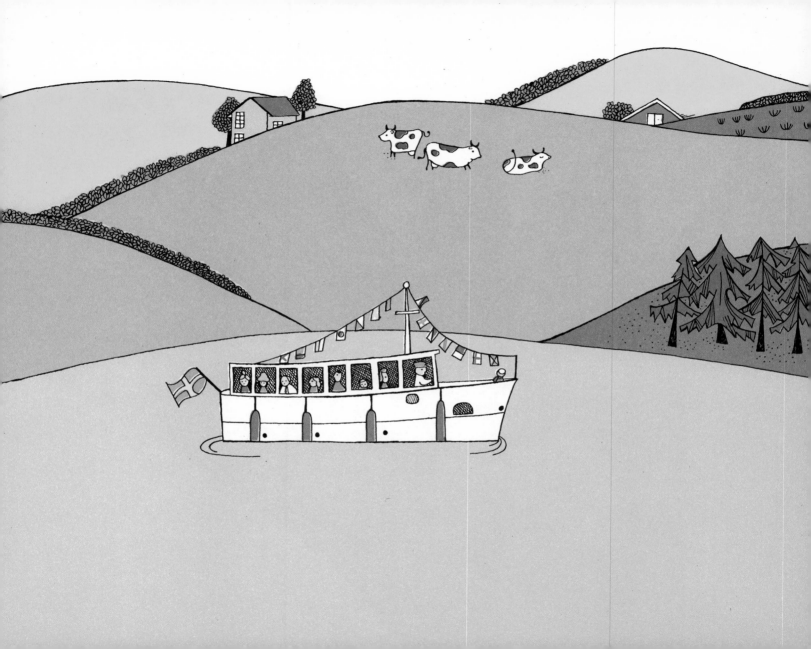

A deer came out of the forest and drank at the edge of the still water.

The boat passed an island where there were birds and rabbits flitting and hopping on the shore.

Eric knew that in this part of Sweden a chain of lakes stretched between the hills and through the valleys. A long time ago a canal had been built to connect these lakes.

The little boat came to the end of the first lake. The channel narrowed until it was just wide enough for the boat to squeeze through. The sides of the channel were old stone walls. Sometimes the fenders brushed against the sides. They shielded the little boat, so her white paint did not get scratched.

Now the little canal boat came to the first lock. The lock was like a great big step that would lower the boat down into the next lake.

Eric had come to the most important part of his job on the boat.

The captain signalled the engineer to stop the boat. As it slowed, Eric jumped off, right onto the land.

There he saw the big wooden handle on top of a stone base. He must turn the handle by walking it around and around. He had practiced this before and he knew it wasn't hard to do. As he turned it, two big wooden gates would swing out from the walls of the canal and close behind the little boat.

Eric took hold of the handle and pushed it. It didn't move!

He pushed again, as hard as he could, but he still couldn't move the handle. The boat's clock was ticking and Eric knew he was taking too much time. He could see the captain looking toward him impatiently. He shut his eyes and strained against the handle with all his weight. But still it didn't budge.

Suddenly he heard the engineer calling to him from his porthole.

"Eric, turn the handle the other way!"

Eric ran around the handle, hurrying. He slipped and almost fell. He grabbed the handle and began pushing it in the other direction. It turned with no trouble at all. Around and around he walked, as fast as he could go, pushing the handle in front of him. The wooden gears squeaked. Then slowly the two wooden gates swung out from the walls and closed behind the little boat.

Eric ran along the wall to a place ahead of the boat, where another set of gates was closed in front of the little boat. Now the boat was enclosed in the lock, with walls on each side and closed gates in front of it and behind it. The lock was like a room—without a ceiling.

Ahead of the boat was another lake, but it was many feet below the lock.

Eric was busy turning a big wheel that stood near the gate handle. As he did this, little doors opened around the gates to let the water go out of the lock. As the water flowed out, the water level in the lock went down and down, and lowered the little boat with it.

The passengers on the after deck could see the gates there getting taller and taller as the water in the lock went lower and lower. Some of them took pictures of the gates.

When the water was down to the same level as the lake ahead, Eric turned the handle and opened the gates in front of the boat. The engineer started the engine again.

Eric jumped back on board and the little boat continued on her way out of the lock into the lake below. Eric had helped the little canal boat to go down a big step!

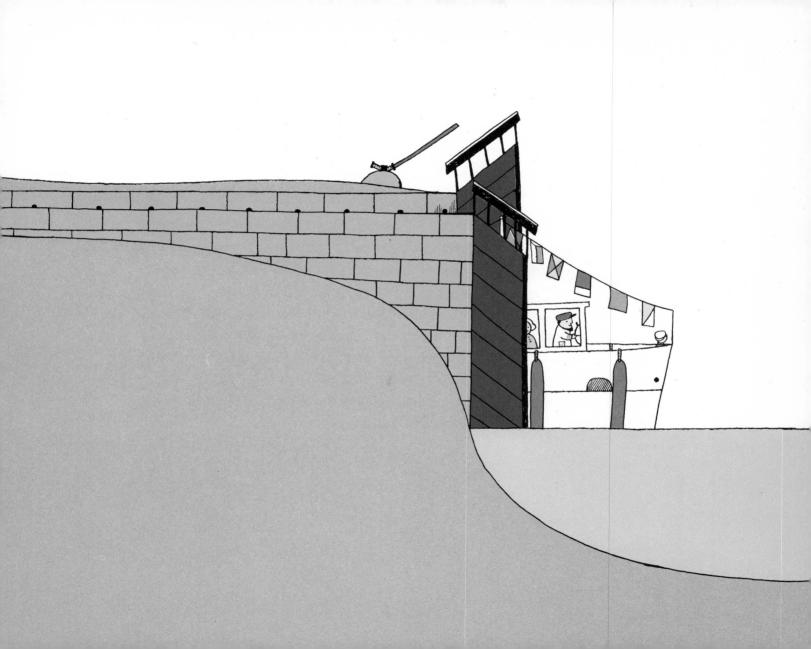

The cook had been busy all morning, and now a delicious smell floated up the stairs and around the whole boat. It was time for Eric to ring the dinner bell. The passengers went down to the dining room. Eric helped serve each one a plate of boiled potatoes and meat loaf and bread and cheese. Eric remembered what the captain had said, and he wanted to do everything that would make the passengers happy. He served them quickly and got extra milk for the thirsty children.

After dinner, the passengers thanked the cook and went back up on deck. Eric helped wash the dishes.

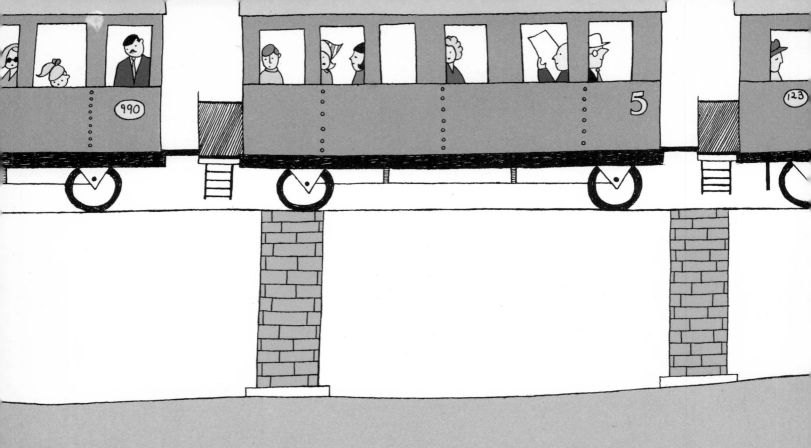

Soon the channel became narrower once more, and here a shiny
green and black train crossed the railroad bridge over the canal.

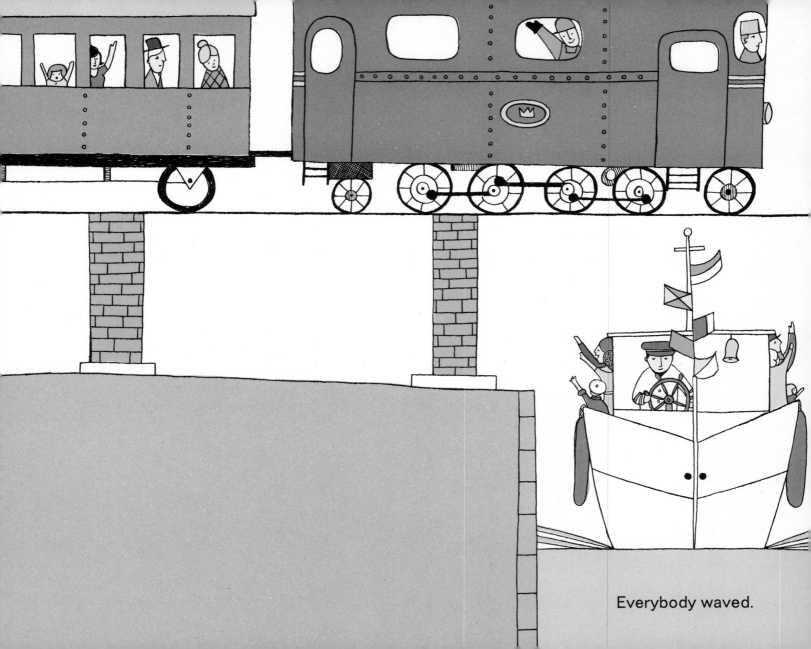

Everybody waved.

Now the passengers knew they were coming to the town and the end of their trip on the little canal boat. They all gathered up their children and their bundles. There was just one more lock to go through.

The little boat was right on time. The passengers were ready to get off. Eric jumped off the boat. In a few steps he was at the handle, ready to close the gates in back of the boat.

But instead of closing the gates, Eric hesitated. He was looking down at the water. The passengers were looking, too, and laughing and taking pictures. A mother duck and her family were swimming along toward the lock.

Eric knew he must be quick about closing the gates, to keep the little boat on time. The captain, who couldn't see what was happening, wondered why Eric was taking so much time to close the gates. He called to Eric.

"Hurry up and shut the gates!"

The minutes were passing. Eric didn't know what to do. He remembered the captain's instructions: THE PASSENGERS MUST ALWAYS BE HAPPY. THE BOAT MUST BE ON TIME. And he heard the captain's angry voice shouting at him again.

But Eric couldn't stop watching the ducks. They looked so little as they hurried toward the lock. The mother duck was saying, "Quack, Quack," encouraging her seven little ducklings to swim faster and to stay together. Eric made up his mind. He would wait for the ducks!

When all the ducks were in the lock, Eric turned the handle and then the gates began to close.

The little ducks bobbed up and down in the water next to the canal boat like little yellow marshmallows. And when the boat continued on her way out of the lock, the duck family was following right behind it.

Now the little canal boat was late.

The captain steered the boat close to the landing. The passengers all got off, laughing and patting Eric on the back as they said good-bye. One of them wanted to take a picture of the captain and Eric from the shore, and the captain agreed. He put his hand on Eric's shoulder and said, "Eric's going to be working on the boat with us all summer."

Eric was surprised. "But I made the boat late," he said.

"Yes, but you made the passengers very happy!" the captain answered, laughing.

And Eric turned and looked at the camera with a great big smile.